Yoanna

Heights of Love Series

Sujeiry Gonzalez

Corner of Press, LLC

Contents

How Did I Get Here?

"Love in an elevator! Lovin' it up 'till I hit the ground!"

I poke my brother, Joel, in the ribs as he begins to whistle the rest of the Aerosmith classic. Only I can't stand this song and its overly sexualized romanticism. Who wants to make love in an elevator while plummeting to their death? And who says "make love" anyway? Not me.

I, Yoanna De Santos, better known as Yo, and soon-to-be Yoanna Rodriguez, am a realist. Joel? He's a former closeted romantic who sprung right out of the closet thanks to his relationship with my best friend, Candi.

"Ugh, you know how much I hate that song, bro!" I cover my ears with my hands and stick my tongue out at Joel.

"You just need some *real* love, sis, to know what it feels like to love someone when shit goes down," Joel throws his head back and laughs, slapping his lap as if he were the opening act at a comedy club.

"I do have real love," I say. "As a matter of fact," I grab my phone from my white Dolce clutch, "let me text Pedro now. He should be here soon."

And when he arrives, I'll show Joel that my relationship with Pedro is just as exciting as his relationship with Candi. We might not suck each other's lips off in public, but our relationship, ahem, *engagement,* is solid. Pedro and I have a stable, committed partnership and soon, marriage. We have our issues. And, yes, we get in relationship ruts, especially when Pedro is in a funk, which lately has felt like an ongoing episode of *Days of Our Lives*, but we're a team.

"Come on, sis! Let's party." Joel interrupts my train of thought.

The elevator doors open and I step out and into my OB-GYN office, decked out in red and gold to celebrate Christmas Eve. I scan the crowd gathered for the annual event, which I now host at my practice instead of Mami's living room in Washington Heights. Inviting family, friends, and colleagues to spend *Noche Buena* inside the business I've built from the ground up at only 30 years old feels good. Well, 31 in two hours.

Yup. I am a Christmas baby. A tough day to be born since everyone is focused on traveling, last-minute gift shopping, Jesus, and who they'll kiss under the mistletoe. It all goes down at midnight, which happens to be my time of birth. That's right. I was born on December 25th at midnight. I am nothing if not a punctual overachiever.

"Hey, baby!" Candi rushes toward us, throwing her entire body on Joel. They go at it, making out right in front of me like I don't exist. But only for a second. As Candi sucks on Joel's lower lip, she reaches for my shoulder and pulls me in, slightly detangling from my twin brother and hugging me tightly with one arm.

"My two favorite people," she gushes. "Come on! Let's take shots before the big announcement."

Candi looks up at Joel, her eyes twinkling. He winks at my best friend in agreement.

"Announcement?" I ask, puzzled. "What are you two keeping from me?"

They beam; cheeks flushed with excitement. Joel nods, giving Candi the go-ahead to reach into her back pocket and slide a 3-carat, halo diamond right on *that* finger.

"Are you two...?" I gasp.

Joel and Candi have only been an item for 5 months. Pedro and I were engaged after 3 years of dating. Maybe this is too fast, but they look *so* happy. I'm not here to rain on their Idealism Parade – at least not today.

"Yo," Joel looks at me with narrow eyes, "don't be negative. We know how you can be with your timelines, but this is me and Candi."

He looks at my best friend and his now fiancé. "This is us." Joel plants a kiss on her forehead. She leans in and rubs her cheek on his.

"We're happy, Yo," Candi assures. "Be happy for us, okay?"

I sigh, nodding my head in agreement although I still have my concerns. Joel and Candi are always jumping into things – relationships, sex, jobs. They aren't steady or methodical like Pedro and I, but I want them to be happy. God, they look *so* happy.

"You have my blessing, okay, babe?" I say to Candi, flashing her a smile. "You both do."

Candi claps, giggling with excitement. "Let's go, baby. Let's tell the world!"

Joel smiles wide, his dimples deepening. I watch them walk through the crowd and onto the mini stage that will later serve as the spotlight for bad karaoke crooning, aside from Candi who can blow like Beyoncé. Unlike Pedro who sounds like a dying frog. Speaking of, where is he? His shift ended two hours ago and he hasn't responded to any of my texts.

"Please don't ruin tonight with your mood," I mumble, grabbing my phone to text my fiancé. I swipe up as Joel and Candi pick up the mic.

"We have something to share with all of you!" Joel begins and passes the mic to Candi.

I scroll through my text messages and see a text from Pedro.

"Joel and I are…" Candi continues where Joel left off.

I click on Pedro's text.

"We're…" Joel and Candi say simultaneously.

"I'm sorry. I'm not coming tonight. I don't want to do this anymore, Yo."

"Engaged!" Joel and Candi shout into the mic in unison.

The crowd roars, throwing "congratulations" and "we knew it!" at the gleeful couple while I stand there, frozen. Because my fiancé just broke up with me minutes before my 31st birthday. Because for the first time in my life, I don't know what's next.

22 Floors

"Happy birthday to you!" Candi sings on stage right after their surprise engagement announcement.

"Happy birthday to youuuuuuuuuuuuuuuuuu!" She points at me as she riffs and adlibs like the superstar she is. All I want to do is disappear.

"Where's a baby emergency when I need one?" I say to myself out loud, praying for a premature labor to bust through the doors like Pedro busted up my perfect life.

"Happy birthday dear Yoooooo!" The crowd cheers for my best friend as she throws her head back and sings her heart out. I don't mind that she gets all the attention. Candi has always craved it. I'd rather stick my head in medical journals and vaginas.

"Happy birthdaaaaaaaay toooooooooooo youuuuuu!" Candi finishes.

"And many more!" Joel leans in and croaks into the mic.

"Baby, you're not off the hook!' Candi gushes. "Your song is in 2 minutes!"

They laugh into the mic and kiss like telenovela protagonists. That means with tongue and tons of passion. I roll my eyes and look away, sensing something I rarely feel – jealousy. As a straight-A, organized, and financially abundant overachiever, I've never felt envious a day in my life. On the contrary, women often wish to emulate my life thanks to my designer wardrobe alone. I crack my neck, releasing the tension I feel creeping up from my spine to my shoulders and, if I don't keep my composure, my temples. Tension headaches are my kryptonite. I don't need one tonight.

The onlookers clap and hoot. This is my chance to make an excuse to get out of here. Because it's my birthday *and* my Christmas party and I'll leave if I want to. And I fucking want to. Questions about Pedro's whereabouts will come crashing any minute now. In typical Dominican fashion, my family will bombard me with side eyes and raised eyebrows because my fiancé isn't here to celebrate my birthday and ring in the holidays with me.

I can hear my mom now. *"Yoanna, ese hombrecito te tiene que tratar mejor."*

I'd nod like the good girl I've always been, agreeing with her that Pedro should treat me better. Never disrespect Mami, I was told. Or your *tia*. So I'll even hold my tongue when Aunt Flor, the family gossip queen, gets wind of my broken engagement. My shocking *noticia* will be headline news in *De Santos en Fuego*, our family Whatsapp Group Chat. No matter how I spin this – and I am great at showcasing my life like a perfectly curated Instagram feed – it's a bad look. I don't want anyone's pity. I take care of people, not the other way around. Victim mode does not look good on me.

Candi commences singing to Joel à la Marilyn Monroe. "They need a private room," I whisper to myself, the green-eyed monster simmering under my biting words. Let me not give them any ideas. They might sneak into one of my patient rooms and bang their brains out. I shudder at the thought. I do not need to imagine my best friend and my twin brother fucking. Although I'm sure the sex is mind-blowing. I mean, look at how they eye each other! They can't wait to rip each other's clothes off. Even at six months, Pedro and I were as cold as a metal speculum.

***

"Babe, I was thinking we can maybe use a vibrator?" I suggested one night when Pedro couldn't get hard.

Pedro often went flaccid when stressed, which happened often due to the pressures of medical residency and the financial burden of supporting his family in the Dominican Republic. Our level-headedness and desire to provide for our loved ones connected us immediately. I wanted to make our relationship work, even if I rarely orgasmed with Pedro. I faked it every time. Not the first time for me, or most women, but still. I wanted to experience 'The Big O' with the man I was determined to marry.

Concerned after a few failed attempts, I asked Pedro to get his testosterone levels checked. I'm a medical professional, after all. Pedro refused. He's as proud as I am; a lethal combination in a relationship. It's also what led me to do something very un-Yo like: I purchased a bullet at The Pleasure Shop, a high-end, adult store in the West Village. Timid and sexually traditional, I knew Pedro would need some convincing. To be honest, so did I. I've never been the adventurous type. I've loosened up thanks to my 20-year friendship with Candi, but I'm careful and methodical in everything that I do. Including sex.

One night while fooling around in bed, I opened my nightstand drawer and grabbed the bullet vibrator and my iPhone. I opened up an article that shared the health benefits of using sex toys. A chubby kid growing up, Pedro's now a health fanatic who works out six days a week. He will do just about anything to keep his body fat at six percent. His body is sick! It's one of the reasons I wanted our sex life to be fantastic. With a body like that, how could it *not* be?

"I don't feel comfortable, Yoanna," Pedro said sternly, as he rubbed my clitoris with his fingers.

"Please...let's just try."

He pulled away.

"Wait. Don't stop."

He folded his arms across his chest and went mute, his go-to strategy to shut me out.

"It was just a suggestion, Pedro."

"A suggestion I don't want to discuss," he replied tersely.

"So that's it. You're done with..." I pointed at my pussy.

"Done. You killed the mood, Yo."

Pedro fluffed his pillow with a punch before rolling to his side. Staring up at the ceiling, I wondered, is Pedro the one? Of course he is, I convinced myself quickly. He's a good man, a doctor, and family-oriented. All the things I need and want in a husband and the father of my children. And with that, I set my sights on Pedro for the long term.

***

I sigh, staring down at Pedro's text message again. "I need to get the fuck out of here."

But how? I turn to my right. With Joel by her side, Candi is showing off her engagement ring to Tia Flor. I can see the headline: *Y ESA PIEDRA*? She's probably interrogating Joel about the cost of Candi's engagement ring. I look down at my left hand. My unimpressive, 1-carat, princess-cut engagement ring only glistens due to my mahogany skin. Pedro is frugal. He settled on the most affordable ring, which I picked out at the jeweler so that we could invest in our financial future.

"It's just a ring," he said matter-of-factly as he handed over his credit card.

"Cheap ass," I say out loud, shuddering at the memory.

I can feel my cheeks burning and my temples throbbing. I crack my neck again and look to my left at the emergency exit, hiding behind a coat rack packed with fake furs, peacoats, and bubble jackets. I inch my way backward and make my way to the door. En route, my cousin Reina stops me to wish me a happy birthday.

"31! Ugh, I'd kill to be that age again," Reina slurs. Her martini swishes in her left hand. At 45 years old, Reina often reminisces about her clubbing days at the Copa, Latin

Quarters, and Jade Terrace. "Speaking of getting older..." Reina continues.

I know what she'll say next. She'll ask if this is the year that I marry Pedro. Before she utters another word, I put my iPhone to my ear.

"Emergency!" I mouth to Reina while pointing at my phone. I kiss her goodbye and step away from her. Reina gets further and further away, swallowed by the crowd that I gathered. As other relatives and friends come toward me I signal to my phone, shaking my hand violently so they know I mean business, which isn't difficult to fake. Business is at the top of my priority list.

I'm finally by the emergency exit. Hand on the knob, I push the door and feel resistance, like a boulder is on the other side. I push harder, using all of my force. I work out four times a week and do Pilates; so I have pretty impressive strength for a 135-pound, five-foot-eight OB-GYN. With one last push, I stumble through the door.

"You're kind of mighty," the stranger in front of me says with a smirk. I let the door slam behind me.

"Not *kind* of. I am," I reply tersely, eyeing him up and down.

Six-foot-two. Golden skin. Five o'clock shadow. Coiled, dirty blonde hair. Large, dark brown eyes. Lips as full as mine. Lean, but strong. His muscles protrude underneath his emerald green shirt, the color illuminating his skin. I swallow hard, unsure of what to say next as his chestnut eyes twinkle with an intense soulfulness.

"Okay, *Mighty*. I'm Benjamin," he says phonetically, in Spanish. "Ben for short."

He extends his hand. I grab it reluctantly. I don't know him. And I know everyone on the guest list. I hold my breath, slightly panicking that I'm in a stairwell with a stranger. Maybe he's a long lost cousin – or worse – a long lost son that's about to confront one of my *tios*. Aunt Flor would love that.

"Who do you know here?" I say, dropping my hand from his grip.

"I don't."

He leans back on the railing behind him and smirks again. I fold my arms in front of me – my power pose – even though I'm freaking out internally. Forget a long-lost son. Ben might just be a *bagamundo* from the street that snuck into the building to get high! I sniff. I don't smell anything suspicious. Shit. Maybe he's a cokehead?

"I'm working. Server." Ben finally says.

"Oh," I say, remembering that I emphatically asked that servers wear green to match my holiday decor.

"Well, why are you out here? I'm not paying you *not* to work," I bite.

"This is your party, huh?" He raises his eyebrows. "Impressive."

"Yes. It's my party. My office. My family. My money that's paying for you to do what exactly?"

"Just taking a break, boss." Ben bows his head and pretends to tip a nonexistent hat on his head.

I clear my throat, startled at his cute gesture. "Well, get back inside," I say all boss-like.

"Can't. You kicked away my entrance plan." He points at a flattened can of Pepsi by the side of the door.

"That's your door stopper?" I snap back.

He shrugs and smirks again. I feel the heat rushing to my cheeks.

I sigh. "Just come downstairs with me. Security can let you back inside."

"Will do, boss." His raspy voice reverberates through my body.

I stomp toward the staircase and down the stairs – Ben behind me – and make my way down 22 floors.

Hot Service

B en trails behind me in silence. I hold my breath, hoping he doesn't make small talk. What would we talk about anyway? Appetizers?

Floor 15.

Ben begins whistling "Back to Black" by Amy Winehouse. I stop mid-step and look back, my eyebrows furrowed in surprised confusion. "You like Amy?" he asks, stopping mid-chorus.

"She's alright," I lie. "Back to Black" is my secret favorite song. Everyone, including Candi, believes it's "Dakiti" by Bad Bunny. Don't get me wrong, I get down like a *tipica Dominicana* to Benito, but "Back to Black" is the song I blast on repeat in my car after a terrible day. "Dakiti" gets me going, but when my head feels like it's about to explode from the pressures of life, family, and Pedro, it's all Amy.

Pedro. My eyes well up with tears. "That bad? I'm sorry. Not a whistle more," Ben teases, trying to lighten the moment.

"No," I whisper, "it's fine. I actually *love* her."

Ben and I lock eyes. He smiles softly before waving his hand in front of me and saying, "Well, lead the way and I'll whistle away."

I turn around and smile for the first time in what feels like hours. As we make it to floor 10, I'm singing along – badly – but in sync with Ben.

"You know you never told me your name." Ben interrupts his whistling.

"Oh," I say, "Yoanna. Yo for short."

"Yo. I like it," Ben says.

I blush a bit but concentrate on the steps ahead. I haven't flirted in so long. And he's definitely flirting with me, right? It feels nice. Especially after being dumped by text by my fiancé. Single at 31. Having to start all over again. Four years of my life wasted. What am I going to do now?

Floor 9.

Overwhelmed, I stop dead in my tracks and lean against the wall.

"What's wrong?" Ben rushes in and stands in front of me.

"I just need a break," I say, holding back tears. "Go ahead, I'll catch up."

"I'm not leaving you." Ben gazes into my eyes. I turn away, afraid of the waterworks.

"Fine," I say, slightly frustrated, yet feeling surprisingly grateful that Ben stayed put. I want to vent and cry – alone. But it feels nice to be supported.

"What do you need?"

I face him and peer into his eyes, full of a tenderness and concern than I rarely felt from Pedro.

"I was dumped by my fiancé tonight. On Christmas Eve. Minutes before my 31st *birthday*." There. I said it. I spoke it into existence. I'm too exhausted to keep it in anymore.

"You don't deserve that. And happy birthday," Ben whispers. He comes in closer, closing the gap between us. His full, pink lips are only inches from the fullness of mine. I look away again, my heart beating a mile a minute.

"You don't even know me. I might be a terrible person." I snort, full of sarcasm as tears roll down my cheeks.

"I assure you that you are not," he says, softly wiping away a tear, his fingertips tracing my cheekbone. "Can I give you a hug?"

He rests his hand on my shoulder. It warms to his touch and I crave this stranger from the stairwell. I give in, locking eyes with him again. Ben opens his arms so I can cocoon myself inside his embrace. I inhale his musk. A blend of amber and citrus. We stand there for what feels like hours before he pulls away. I don't want him to pull away.

"Shall we?" Ben bows again and waves his hand toward the stairs. I giggle.

"Mission accomplished," he says with a smile.

"Mission?" I ask.

"To make you smile, boss."

I smile wider, exposing my straight white teeth. Just like that the tension leaves my shoulders, neck, and temples. We continue to make our way downstairs, only this time we walk side by side. I tell Ben about my awful relationship with Pedro and he empathizes, shaking his head from time to time as if to say, "You didn't deserve that." He shares more about himself as well. How his high school sweetheart broke his heart when she cheated on him with his best friend. How he gave up on love for a long time because of it and is now ready to try again.

"I'm finally open to meeting someone and giving it my all," Ben says with a sheepish smile. His sudden vulnerability sends my heart and my pussy into overdrive. I feel her getting wetter by the minute.

"That's...sweet," I manage to say.

Floor 3.

"Tell me about your family," I say, increasingly curious.

"My mom is Dominican and I never met my dad. He bounced back to Germany before I was born. He and my mom met in Puerto Plata at the hotel she worked for. You know how European men love to find a Dominican girl, use them up, and leave..." His voice trails. I find myself at a loss for words.

"It's all good. My mom struggled for a while but remarried when I was five. He's Nuyorican, brought us to the States, and raised me. He's my father by all accounts."

We make our way down the last flight of steps. I stop and rest my hand on Ben's back.

"Thank you for sharing."

Ben steps in closer. My back leans against the cold, concrete wall as he presses his chest against mine.

"She'd love you," he whispers, lips grazing mine.

"We should go." I lick my lips, my tongue making contact with his.

"Hello? Who's there?"

"Security."

I gently push Ben away from me. He takes a few steps back and we make our way down to the first floor.

"Hi!" I say, coming around the corner. "It's Dr. De Santos!"

"Are you okay, ma'am?" Marcos, the security guard, eyes Ben before locking eyes with me.

"Yes, yes."

Marcos pushes the door wide open and I'm met with a brisk winter gust that almost knocks me off my Red Bottoms.

"Ooooh!" I scream, finally outside.

Ben grabs me by the waist, holding me steady. "It's a cold one."

Suddenly, it feels like a steamy NYC day.

"Yes." I clear my throat. "My car," I mumble, "it's that way." I point to the garage to my left.

"Let's go then," Ben says.

"No. I'm good. It's just right there," I reply, summoning some composure. "I can walk by myself. It's safe."

"So...we trudge through 22 flights of stairs together, pour our guts out, and you expect me to leave you to walk to your car alone? That's not happening, Yo."

Ben crosses his arms, defending his position. Despite my knee-jerk response to keep up my tough girl act, my lips curl into a half-smile. I'm not used to being taken care of. A doctor and the responsible twin, I've always buried my head in the sand and ignored the chaos. I've thrived because of it. Push away the sadness, babe, I've said to myself more times than I can count. The exemplary daughter never gets a break to break down.

"Fine." I roll my eyes, pretending my heart isn't beating out of my chest. I can hear it pulsating in my ears. I feel myself burning up again. Like it's summer in winter and I have way too many clothes on. Am I in early, *early* menopause? Is this what 31 feels like or is this uncharacteristic urge to rip my clothes off because of Ben?

He smiles. "Lead the way then."

I nod and walk briskly next door to the car garage, maintaining a few feet of distance between Ben and I. I feel like it's 102 degrees outside despite the wind whipping my black, pressed tresses all over my face.

"This is me," I say, pointing to my black, sleek Audi Coupe.

"She is a beauty," he whistles, tracing his fingertips on the hood.

I shiver and stand back, watching him admire Bonita. I named her Bonita (Spanish for beautiful) because she is a gorgeous piece of machinery, and my pride and joy.

I'm a car freak thanks to my dad, a retired mechanic who spent more time on the road looking for car parts than at home. My mother held it down though. After work-ing eight-hour shifts and four hours of overtime, she still managed to cook next day's dinner every night. I got my strength and resilience from her. I learned to cook, clean, and keep a nice and tidy home. I had no other choice. Joel, the man of the house, just sat and watched. Typical Latino macho shit. He was raised to be El Principe while I ran around like Cinderella. Thanks to me, he turned it around after high school. Joel only applied to college after I caught him smoking weed in the stairwell of our apartment building, and I threatened to tell our parents.

"Here are your choices," I threatened. "I tell Mami and Papi and you're banished to the Dominican Republic to live with *abuela en el campo*, or I keep your little habit a secret and you let me help you apply to college."

"You mean your rules, sis." He rolled his eyes and put out his blunt.

"Exactly, babe. So what's it going to be?"

"An education it is," Joel sighed.

By the following week, Joel had applied to six colleges of my choice. This smartypants, pain-in-the-ass twin brother of mine got accepted to every single school. He chose to attend NYU for marketing. Joel won't admit it, but I saved his ass and positioned him to have the fabulous marketing career he now boasts about.

***

"What are you smiling about?" Ben says, knocking me out of my reverie.

"I was just thinking about the day I got the keys," I fib. Ben doesn't need to know anything else about my life. He's a stranger that I will never see again.

"Well, it's impressive," Ben says, taking steps toward me. "Just like you."

Ben's fingers slither from the hood of my car up to my face. He grabs a strand of hair stuck to my nude lipgloss and tucks it away behind my ear.

I clear my throat. "I have to go." Although I really want to stay.

"So go."

Ben smirks again, his coffee browns twinkling with just a hint of mischief. He leans in closer, inches away from my lips. I can feel the warmth of his breath on my flushed cheeks. I part my lips as he cocks his head and sucks my upper lip, his tongue intertwining with mine softly and slowly. I wrap my hands around his neck and tug at the hair at the nape of his neck.

"Hmmm," I moan.

"You're so beautiful," Ben whispers.

His hands unbutton my double-breasted Dolce coat. I feel a shiver as the brisk air hits my dark chocolate skin. Ben sheds his black Nautica puffer jacket. He grabs me again, clutches my tight ass, and lifts me off the floor. I yelp excitedly when Ben sits me down on the hood of Bonita. I wrap my long, mahogany legs around his waist. Ben moves his tongue from my mouth to my neck, sucking every inch as he moves down to my clavicle. He buries his head in my Double D's. I pump my pelvis and gyrate my ass all over Bonita, arching my back and opening my legs. Ben locks eyes with me before ripping off my netted stockings with his hands. He yanks my black La Perla thong to the side. His fingers dance with my clit, rubbing softly and slowly at first.

"Faster," I groan.

Ben obeys. His fingers pick up the pace as his tongue ravishes mine.

"Ooooh!" I yell, unable to control my moans.

"I want you so bad," Ben croons.

Dropping on his knees, he spreads my legs wider and devours her. Penetrating me with his digits and wet, warm tongue, I gasp, pumping my pelvis in unison with his fingers, slow and steady.

"Ah, ah, ah!" I scream into the night.

"Yoanna," Ben whispers, thrusting his fingers deeper and deeper inside my wet pussy as his thumb massages my clit. I fall back onto Bonita in a haze of ecstasy, whimpering as I get closer to orgasm.

Ben dives in deeper."That's it. Come for me, *bella*."

I writhe like a cat in heat. He stands up, flips me over, and I get on all fours. Ben flicks my left nipple with his other hand while his fingers keep pumping into me from behind. My Double D's bounce. I swerve my ass slowly and sensually as if grinding to a bachata.

"I love this," Ben moans, kissing my back. His right thumb caresses my nub and I fall onto Bonita, my chest pressed against smooth steel. He sticks his tongue in my pussy from behind, ravishing me.

"Oh, oh, ooooooh!" I hear myself squealing. "Aaaaaaaaaaaah!" I yell, orgasming for what feels like the first time in my life. I squirm on top of Bonita as Ben decorates my back with kisses. He falls beside me, breathing heavily, his mouth dripping with my juices. We lock eyes. This all feels so primitive, so out of control, so un-Yo like. And yet here I am relishing in it.

Fast Escape

"**I** watched you all night," Ben whispers.

"What does that mean?" I say defensively, pulling down my dress.

Ben crosses his brows confused. "How could I not? Look at you."

"Ok." I clear my throat and slide off of Bonita. I snatch my belongings off the floor.

Ben shoots up and climbs off of Bonita. "What's wrong?"

I feel uncomfortable with being watched, babe, I want to bark. Did he know who I was this entire time? That I own my practice and hosted this party? That I have enough money to buy this car outright?

"This was a mistake," I bite. I throw my coat over my shivering body.

"What did I say?" Ben reaches for my shoulder with one hand. I flinch. He drops his arm and steps back.

"I have to go," I respond. Keys in hand, I unlock the door.

"Wait. You're not going to give me your number after all that?" He signals to the hood of the car.

"I don't think that's a good idea." I rush through the sentence.

"And why is that?" Ben asks, searching for answers to my sudden harshness. He cocks his head to the side confidently, awaiting my reply.

"We're just...*different,*" I say coldly.

"You're Dominican. I'm Dominican. You're from the Heights and so am I. We're both 31. We're obviously..." Ben points to Bonita's hood again, the scene of our passionate, toe-curling, orgasmic rendezvous, "vibing." Ben's lips curl into a half smile as he finishes his sentence.

I inhale slowly, resisting the urge to push him into the front seat, rip his pants off, and ride him until sunrise. No. I can't trust him. He's been "watching" me. He's a creep, babe, I convince myself. A creep with nothing to offer.

"Look," I say. "I appreciate your help in the stairwell and..." I signal to the hood with my chin because I can't bear to speak about what just transpired. "But this is where it ends."

Ben's shoulders slump. He stuffs his hands in his pockets and I open my car door, sliding into the black leather seat. I turn on my seat warmers even though the flame Ben lit inside of me still simmers within. I press the accelerator, my engine roaring, and back out of my parking spot. From my review mirror, I watch as Ben tips his hand to his head again and mouths, "You got it, boss."

***

I ride the elevator up to my condo. A wave of tension creeps from the bottom of my head and up to my temples. For a brief, orgasmic moment, I forgot about the shitstorm that is my life. Now it's time to face reality.

Bing! The doors open to the 22nd floor. I walk down the long corridor toward my condo and unlock the door to my 3-bedroom, 2-bath apartment tucked inside a luxurious building on Fort Washington Avenue. Despite my success and desire for the finer things in life, I could never leave The Heights. This neighborhood grounds me, and I love working with local patients. I stumble upon them and their babies at the grocery store, the bodega, the beauty supply store, and on occasion, as I quickly shop for cheap, raggedy heels for Candi on 181st Street. She refuses to let me buy her fancy footwear.

"It makes me feel like a charity case, Yo. You already help me with my rent," she whined when I presented her with a pair of pink studded Louboutins.

"These are the Duvette Spikes. You were eyeing them on Instagram." I shoved the beautiful Red Bottoms in her face. "You can't resist them, babe."

Candi grabbed them, inhaled dramatically, and shoved them back into the bag. "No. But thank you."

"Fine. Keep your cheap shoes." I stuck my tongue out at her in jest, secretly wishing she'd change her mind.

***

I love taking care of Candi as if she were my daughter, even though we're the same age. Raised by a single mom making ends meet, pursuing a singing career in a whitewashed market, and before Joel, engaging in a string of toxic situationships, Candi's had it rough. I adore her and always love making her happy with the one thing I know she usually can't resist: shoes. Until the day when she decided to take a stand. Secretly, I felt proud of her for fending for herself. Even though I still chip in on rent when she's more strapped for cash than usual. Although, that's Joel's responsibility now.

"Candi and Joel," I whisper as I walk into my massive apartment. "God, I can't believe they're engaged."

I look down at my phone. Twenty missed calls and five text messages. One reads in all caps: PRESS 1 IF YOU'RE IN DANGER! In my desperate need to escape my party, I forgot to tell my best friend and twin brother that I'm safe. Utterly embarrassed and sexhausted…but safe.

"Not really heartbroken though," I realize as I hang my coat on a hook and walk toward the kitchen. "You dodged a bullet, babe." I admit to myself while opening the liquor cabinet. I grab a bottle of Prosecco with one hand and a glass flute with the other and pour to the rim. "Pedro was exhausting."

I kick off my white, Hot Chick Red Bottoms and lean against the kitchen island, taking slow and steady sips. I look down at my phone and find Candi's number.

"Yo! OH MY GOD! Are you okay? We've been so worried! Can you talk? Cough if you're in danger!" Candi rattles on, screeching in my ear.

"If you'd let me get a word in, babe, you'd know I'm perfectly ok." *Well, not exactly,* I think as I walk into my bedroom and stare at Pedro's empty closet. He even took my satin hangers with him.

"Cheap bastard," I grunt into the phone.

"Pedro? Did something happen to him? Was *he* kidnapped?! Are they asking for ransom?" Candi continues to spin the drama. She watches way too many *telenovelas*.

"Pedro and I..." I swallow hard. "We broke up. He..broke it off. Tonight."

"That fucking asshole!" Candi shouts. "Yo, I'm so sorry. I'm still at the party, but I'm coming over, okay?"

I hear Candi calling Joel.

"No, Candi, wait!" I say. "Don't tell Joel yet."

"Of course. He's my fiancé but you're my Day 1. You're my best friend, Yo. Whatever you need is what you'll get."

"Thanks, babe."

I sigh, thankful that Candi is still in my corner despite being engaged to Joel. Joel will find out when I'm ready to face the music known as my family. He's never liked Pedro and, although he and I are close and he loves and supports me, Joel can be a bit of a know-it-all. Even more so when vodka is coursing through his veins. I don't need him to rub this in my face right now.

"See you soon!" Candi shouts over music before hanging up the phone.

I continue to inspect my condo. Thank God I purchased it alone. Prudent is my middle name. No. Really. My full name is Yoanna Prudencia De Santos. Awful. But it must have shaped my personality somehow. When Pedro moved in, I never put his name on the lease. What's in a name? Everything, apparently.

I fall back onto my King-sized bed and spread my arms like I'm making a snow angel. I stare at the ceiling and breathe, allowing my body to fully relax since that fantastic and unforgettable orgasm.

"Forget him," I command. "I will never see him again."

Although, I can inquire about him with the catering service. For years, they've catered my events, and I pay them handsomely, including tipping their servers and bartenders much more than the standard 20 percent fee. The owner, Juan, is a distant cousin of Candi's. He would happily provide me with any information I asked for, including Ben's background check and contact information.

"Then I'd have to tell Candi what happened," I remember. Her family is as gossipy as mine. Surely, Juan would let it spill that I asked for a server's phone number. I'd like to keep what happened with Ben to myself.

"So, that's that," I state matter-of-factly.

I turn my head and stare at Pedro's empty closet, feeling a pang of sadness for the first time since I cried with Ben in the stairwell. I close my eyes and feel my shoulders and neck soften. My body melts into the bed. A tear rolls down my cheek as the fear of the unknown closes in.

***

"What you need now is an adventure!" Candi says as she bursts into my condo and throws her arms around my neck. She covers my cheek with kisses, her red lip gloss sticking to my skin.

"What I need now is a napkin," I joke.

She raspberries my cheek and I playfully push her away. Candi topples back and almost falls to the floor. I grab my clumsy best friend's arm, catching her just in time.

"My hero!" Candi sighs, giggling as she finds her footing again. "But, really, *how are you?*"

I shrug. "Aside from the shock that he dropped the bomb on my birthday, I feel okay, babe."

Candi rubs my shoulder and cocks her head to the side. "You seem...different."

I bite my lip, still unsure if I should tell Candi that I received cunnilingus from a stranger on the hood of my car mere minutes after being dumped by my fiancé. I know Candi won't judge me. On the contrary, she'll celebrate my newfound freakiness by hollering at the top of her lungs, "You finally had some fun!" I wouldn't put it past her to haphazardly organize a 'Yoanna's Big O' Happy Hour at our favorite local bar, Vivere.

And it *was* good. My breath quickens as I remember his fingers and tongue. My pussy pulsating as I orgasmed. His fingers slowly and steadily caressing my clitoris from behind.

"Yo. Hello? Are you listening to me?"

"Sure, babe."

"Yay! It's settled. You're going on a date with Juan! I'll text him that you're," Candi winces before finishing that sentence, "recently single. I can tell he has such a crush on you!"

Before I can interject, Candi types a message to Juan and hits send. My phone buzzes instantly.

"Hey, Yo! How'd you like to spend some of your birthday having dinner with me?"

I read Juan's text and sigh, looking up at Candi who is nodding excitedly. What do I have to lose?

"Sure," I text back. "Let's do it."

***

I yawn, stretch my long limbs, and rub the exhaustion from my eyes. Right across from me, I see a photo of Pedro tacked onto my bedroom door and covered in darts. Candi and I stayed up until 4 am drinking Prosecco and attacking Pedro's face with his set of darts, the only thing he left behind. As the last dart landed on Pedro's Roman nose, Candi took an Uber back to her and Joel's place, which is only a mile south of my condo.

"Take that!" Candi hollered, laughing so hard she sloshed Prosecco all over my Frette bedspread, the staple bedding at Waldorf Astoria hotels.

"I never liked his nose," I mused, ignoring a mess for the first time in my life. "It was so...pointy." I took a sip after my observation.

"Pointy can be good in *so* many ways." Candi smiled wide, closed her eyes, and violently shook her head from side to side, simulating nose cunnilingus.

"You're disgusting, babe." I laughed, rolling my eyes jokingly, but secretly wondering what Ben could do with his nose.

My phone buzzes, snapping me out of my daydream. I wrestle with the sheets and grab it, reading Juan's text.

"Confirming dinner for tonight. 6 p.m."

Oh, yes. *That.*

I sigh, stare at the ceiling, and melt into my sheets.

"Just go," I say to myself. "It's just a date. And he's cute and successful."

I close my eyes and focus on my breathing. "Relax. You have an amazing life, your life is perfect," I affirm.

As I drift into a meditative state, Ben's sly smile flashes across my mind. My breathing deepens and I slip into a trance. I can feel the pressure of Ben's hard chest on top of me. I breathe harder, almost panting, and I slide my hand under my nightie, past my belly button, and graze my throbbing pussy. My fingers find my clit. I shut my eyes tighter, imagining that my long and slender fingers are Ben's large, slightly calloused hands. I thrust my pussy forward, arching my back and moaning as I insert two digits inside my bud.

"Oh, Ben," I cry softly, my fingers diving in deeper and thrusting faster while my thumb caresses my clitoris.

"Shit," I squeal, my muscles tightening. "Aaaaaaaaaaaaaaaaaaaah!" My body vibrates, gyrating as I release. I roll over to my side, tighten my legs, and do a kegel to intensify the sensation.

I open my eyes, out of breath. "What has come over me?"

"Ben," I admit to myself. "I, Yoanna De Santos, am officially sprung."

Run In

I run my fingers through my long, pressed tresses and tuck a loose strand behind my ear. My breasts topple over my black, lace La Perla demi-cup bra. I step into the matching black thong followed by my red, Dolce tulle, calf-length dress; its volcanic red hue perfectly complementing my mahogany skin.

"Not bad for 31," I whisper to my reflection in the mirror. This tight, see-through number might give Juan a heart attack.

"Thank goodness I'm a doctor," I giggle at my joke.

Despite agreeing to this birthday date arbitrarily, Juan has always piqued my curiosity. He is a successful and financially stable business owner and a respected member of the community. Juan caters all local events with his team of chefs, servers, vendors, and bartenders. Similar to me, he's kind of a local celebrity. He's the type of man I should date, unlike Ben.

"Ugh, stop it already," I reprimand myself. I shake my head, attempting to get that man out of my system and my irrational desire to taste his luscious lips again.

"Juan and I are a fit," I say, standing firm in my decision. "We can be the Bey and Jay of Washington Heights."

I chuckle as I slip my arms into my black faux fur. Making my way toward the living room, I grab my gold-studded clutch and snatch my iPhone from the charging station. I swing the door open and lock up with my passcode while scrolling through happy birthday texts. I respond to Candi's, "Go get 'em bday girl!" with a kissy face emoji while strutting down the corridor toward the elevator.

"Birthday drinks at Vivere after!" Candi responds.

I press the elevator button with one hand while texting back, "Of course, babe." I continue to scroll, only answering texts from those who are closest to me.

"*Pendejo*," I murmur when it dawns on me that Pedro doesn't even have the *cojones* to wish me a happy birthday.

Bing!

"Going down?" a familiar voice calls as the elevator doors open.

I look up from my phone and come face to face with Ben. Startled, I leap back and stumble, my pink, patent leather stilettos giving out from under me. Ben grabs my elbow just in time while leaning against the elevator doors to keep them from closing. His touch sends shock waves through my body. I feel my legs trembling. I can feel my jaw twitching, rendering me speechless. I'm afraid that if I open my mouth to say something...anything...I won't make it to my date with Juan.

"You ok?" Ben asks, peering into my eyes like a hawk.

I let out a breathless, "Yes," still struggling to find my composure.

"Then come on in."

Ben slides his hand down from my elbow and clasps his hand in mine, pulling me gently toward him. I glide inside the elevator and stand in front of him, the doors closing behind us. Here we are, face to face. Twenty-four hours after he ravaged my pussy.

"Love in an elevator," Ben begins to sing, whistling the rest of the chorus before murmuring, "Happy birthday again, Yo." A confident smile spreads across his face.

I swallow hard, my heart racing and beating so loudly I can hear it in my ears. His russet brown eyes search mine for any sign of connection and heat. I look away and stare at the elevator panel, taking in a quick breath to calm my nerves. I've been watching you all night, his words echo in my mind. Now he's in my building?

"What are you doing here?" I ask boldly, snapping my face back to face him.

I pull my hand away from his and take a step back, crossing my arms, trying to demonstrate to Ben how unpleased I am with him. Actually, I am appalled. How dare he get my contact information and show up where I live?

Bing!

The elevator doors open. A handful of residents wait to hop in. Ben greets them hello as we walk out of the elevator. He turns to me, smiles, and says, "I live here, boss."

I stare at him, frozen in my place, my eyes as wide as saucers. I watch Ben saunter off, whistling the rest of the Aerosmith classic that Joel loves so much as the elevator doors close behind me.

The Proposition

I sit across from Juan with a smile plastered on. I'm shaking on the inside, thanks to my run-in with Ben, but I refuse to let him ruin the rest of my birthday or this date.

I live here, boss.

Ugh, get out of my head! Focus on Juan, who is as handsome as always. At 45 years old, his flawless dark chocolate skin still glistens thanks to that melanin, genetics, and weekly facials. Juan posts his comings and goings on Instagram like it's his job. I did a little pre-date digging, especially since he's only Candi's third cousin. Born and raised in the Dominican Republic, Juan immigrated to NYC at 25, so he and Candi don't know each other very well. They mostly engage at quarterly family reunions. Plus, there's the 15-year age gap.

"He might as well be a stranger," Candi said the night before as she stood crouched on my bed, positioning herself to hit Pedro right on the forehead.

"Damn!" she called when the dart bounced off the wall before falling on her back.

"But he's my blood, so he's fabulous!" Candi waved her arms all over her body to emphasize her fabulosity. "Go get 'em, tiger!"

Now, here I am, ignoring my burning desire for Ben and trying *not* to ask Juan about his recent trip to the Dominican Republic. So he doesn't think I'm a stalker. His company hosted a pro-bono fundraiser for an orphanage in Santiago. He posted photos of the entire thing on the 'Gram in addition to pics of him frolicking on the beach with his team. From Puerto Plata to Las Terranas to Samana, Juan exposed his bronze, broad chest, and pecs all over social media. I'm a bit more low profile. I mostly post photos of babies I've delivered and the local events I attend to promote my business and give back to my community. No bikini selfies in sight. Although my abs are fantastic.

"You look great, Yoanna," Juan says with a slight Spanish accent. "And happy birthday!"

"Thank you," I reply, loosening my shoulders a bit. This is going to be great, I think, continuing my internal pep talk.

"Anything to drink?" The male server stands by Juan's side with a pad in hand. Juan slightly shifts in his seat.

"Ladies first," Juan motions to me with a wave.

The server glares at Juan, towering over him. Juan's shoulders tense. The server then turns to me with a forced, closed smile. His chiseled jaw is as tight as his black jeans. "So, my dear, what will you have to drink?"

"A prosecco, please," I say. "What's your name by the way?"

I always ask for the names of service workers. To show respect. And to file a complaint with their manager if needed. I need my food to arrive hot and for my check to be handed to me when I am ready to go, not two hours after I've asked due to the laissez-faire attitude in most establishments in Washington Heights.

The server faces Juan again and raises one eyebrow. "You can ask *him*."

Juan's eyes look like they're going to burst from their sockets. Before he can say anything, the server takes a step back and says, "I'll be back with your Prosecco, dear, and *your* Sex on the Beach. It's his favorite, you know."

He spins on his heel and walks toward the bar.

"I take it you're a regular here," I say, trying to make light of an uncomfortable situation.

"Yes, yes." Juan clears his throat and wipes his sweaty brow, despite it being the middle of winter.

"So, Yoanna, what are you looking for?"

Juan reaches across the table to graze my hand. I snatch it back, his gesture catching me off guard. I feel like I just witnessed a lover's quarrel, and he's making moves on me and asking about *my* intentions?

"I'm just getting out of a relationship," I state matter-of-factly. "Honestly, I may not want anything but a friend right now," I lie. I definitely wasn't just friends with Ben last night.

"Ok. Good," Juan sighs and slouches back in his chair.

Well, damn. Thanks for the ego boost, babe, I think.

"I have a proposition for you." Juan peers over his shoulder and leans in closer, as if the restaurant is bugged and we're in a *007* flick.

"I'm going to come clean. Lawrence," he motions with his head back at the server who is grabbing our cocktails at the bar, "we are...a *thing*." Juan spits out.

I peer over Juan's shoulder at Lawrence and then stare back at Juan. Immediately, I am relieved that Juan and I can be just friends. I'm not ready for anything as serious as what Juan and I could have been if he weren't into men.

"So," I say, my fingers interlaced in front of me, "does Candi know you're gay?"

"Shhh!" Juan hisses. "Please, don't tell anyone. I...I..." He wipes his brow again, sweat beads now trickling down his temple.

"It's ok, babe. Really." I reach for his right hand and clasp it in mine. "I know how difficult it is to come out in our community. I won't say a word."

"Not even to Candi?" Juan whispers. He grips my hand a little tighter.

"Not even to Candi." I squeeze back to assure him.

"But..." Juan grimaces, hesitating to speak. "My proposition."

I raise one perfectly shaped eyebrow.

"You and me...pretending for a bit?"

I open my mouth to speak but Juan cuts me off.

"I know it's insane to ask this of you."

"It really is, Juan," I say, dropping his hand and leaning back in my chair. I'm all for being supportive, but I'm no one's beard.

"I have a huge event coming up in the Dominican Republic. The Politicos y Artistas Gala."

"Yes, I've heard of it."

The Politicos y Artistas Gala is an extravagant, over-the-top auction where Dominican politicians, actors, singers, musicians, and influencers hobnob. They prance around in their designer attire, flaunting their wealth and connections. I love donning my Dolce and Red Bottoms, but The Politicos y Artistas Gala is too bougie even for me. Inauthentic conversations grate on my nerves.

"Reporters will be there. They constantly ask questions about my....relationship status." Juan picks up a fork and pretends it's a microphone. "Juan! Juan!" he says animatedly. "When are you going to get married? Where are you hiding this woman? Why are you still single?"

He drops the fork and frowns, shaking his head.

"People are starting to gossip. You know how our *cultura* is, Yoanna. They won't accept me if I come out, and this gala places me and Juantastic Events on the radar of every *politico y artista* on the island. Please help me."

Juan finally takes a breath. I cock my head to the side and sigh.

"When is this gala?" I just can't say no to a person in need, even if it puts me in a compromising position.

"Next week. All expenses paid."

"I'm in," I sigh.

Juan's frown literally turns upside down. He clasps his hands in front of his face.

"Thank you, thank you, thank you. You won't regret this."

"I better not," I say, sealing my Beard Contract with a handshake.

Where the Party At?

"Finally! You're here!" Candi throws her arms around my neck, covering my cheek with kisses. "Ok, ok," I giggle. "Let the festivities begin!"

I sigh, trying to muster some energy after my "date" with Juan. But a promise is a promise, and I intend to keep it.

It shouldn't be a problem. When it comes to secrets I'm a steel vault. I never told Joel that two years ago Candi almost slept with cousin Reina's now ex-man, Peter. I caught them making out in Mami's closet at our annual Mother's Day dinner. In typical De Santos family fashion, my relatives turned a classy, catered affair into a *merengue* fest, ripe with Brugal shots and a Presidente beer contest. Needless to say, they trashed the white, minimalist centerpieces that a local florist arranged meticulously for me. I was so frustrated with my relatives' disregard for my pristine planning that I snuck into Mami's bedroom for a breather. That's when I heard Candi giggling.

"Candi and Peter?!" I screamed as I yanked open the closet door.

"Hey, Yo!" Candi smiled innocently from ear to ear, her thick legs sprawled over his thighs.

"Please don't tell Reina!" Peter blurted, pushing Candi off him before jumping out of the closet and racing past me.

"You are *so* dirty, Peter!" I yelled at him, chasing him out of my mother's bedroom before turning back to Candi.

"Why are you so messy, babe?" I said exasperated.

"I don't get it." Candi looked up at me, still sitting on the closet floor.

"That's Reina's man! And now...."

I began to pace, unsure of how to handle a situation between my best friend and my closest first cousin. Candi had no idea who Peter was. Reina kept him tucked away due to her raging trust issues. Because Peter is a dirty *perro*. He cheated on Reina throughout their entire relationship. High school sweethearts, Reina had a difficult time walking away even though Peter never deserved her beautiful and exuberant energy.

"Oh no. No, no, no, no, no, no!" Candi yelled while covering her face. "I didn't know, I promise!" She looked up at me with her big brown eyes, welling up with tears as they often do.

"I know, I know. You would *never*," I reassured her. "I'll take care of it, babe."

"How?" Candi asked earnestly.

"I won't say a word."

Eventually, Reina did find out. But that's a story for another day.

***

"Come on, Yo!" Candi pulls on my hand. We walk toward the back of Viveve toward the garden, which is heated and covered under a plastic dome during winter months.

"Close your eyes!" Candi says.

"Do I have to?" I groan. "It's not a surprise, babe. I know this is my birthday party."

"Just hush and do as I say!" Candi commands.

I glare at her jokingly, surprised at her demanding tone.

"Pleaaaaase!"

That's the Candi I know and love. She can roar as loud as a lion, but she's just a little pussy cat.

"Ok. Surprise me."

Candi leads me into the garden and I instantly hear Joel's loud laugh and Candi shushing him. She squeezes my hand before whispering, "Open!"

I do as I'm told and take in my surroundings. It's a winter wonderland. It's perfect.

"Thank you!" I gush at Candi.

"Anything for you, bestie. You deserve this and so much more. Including my cousin, Juan! You have to tell me everything, but first, let's party!"

I begin to make my rounds with Candi dancing beside me. Joel grabs her from behind and smothers her with kisses before hooking my arm in his.

"Happy birthday again, sis."

"Happy birthday again, bro."

I plant a kiss on his cheek and smile at my twin. He's so happy it fills me with so much joy.

I continue to greet everyone with hugs, kisses, and thank yous. My cousin Reina, a party animal since dumping Peter a year ago, rushes in from the dance floor and yanks at my arm.

"Where the party at, *prima*?! Let's go!" Reina shouts over the music, swerving her wide hips quickly as a *merengue ripiao* plays. I laugh and join her, allowing her to spin me around so fast I almost fall on my stilettos.

"You're losing your moves, *prima*?"

"I could never keep up with you, babe."

Candi joins us on the dance floor. Reina seethes at her, glaring at Candi with her dark gray eyes, before teetering away on her high-heeled combat boots.

"I'll catch you at the bar, Yo," she snaps as she gives Candi a once over.

Despite her innocence, Reina has never forgiven Candi. She resents having to see her at every family function, even more so now that Joel and Candi are an item. It's a reminder of the straw that broke the camel's back between her and Peter. Reina has also managed to keep this from our relatives. Mostly so Aunt Flor doesn't drop the news in the De Santos En Fuego WhatsApp group. She wanted to save herself from the embarrassment of Peter cheating on her with a woman half her age for the umpteenth time.

"Now that Reina and her wrath are gone, how was your date with my *primo*? Tell me!" Candi yells.

"It was good, babe," I lie. "I'll tell you about it later."

Although I promised Juan I wouldn't say a word, I'm not quite sure how I'll keep this from Candi. We never keep secrets from each other. Now, I'm two for two: my romp with Ben and Juan's closeted life as a gay man.

"I need to use the restroom."

I run back inside to Vivere's main room, turn the corner to the bathroom, and come crashing into Ben.

"You," I say, my mind swirling, as he catches me in his arms.

"Yes. Still me." Ben smirks, his lips inches from mine.

I close my eyes and breathe him in as his supple lips make contact. I allow him to devour me all over again.

Who Are You?

"Why are you *everywhere*?" I question, breathing heavily, taking Ben's tongue inside of my mouth.

"Shush," he commands.

Ben kicks the men's bathroom door open with the back of his leg. His hands grip my waist, leading me inside. He locks the door behind us. I jerk my head up at him to stare into his eyes. My chest rises and falls quickly against his. Despite Vivere's pristine restroom, I'd usually be disgusted by this very situation. Offended even. Maybe it's the three rounds of Prosecco I had with Juan, but I want Ben inside of me right here, right now. I felt the fire raging the instant Ben told me to shush. So un-Yo like. All of this is.

With Pedro, I took control of everything. He was terrible at saving money and never initiated sex. I was used to it. Growing up, I always organized Mami and Papi's finances. I still pay their bills online despite their protests about online identity fraud. As for sex with Pedro, I often jumped him and rode him until the cows came home, working my ass off to get off. I purchased my condo on my own despite the naysayers. Mostly Mami who thought I'd emasculate Pedro by buying property before him. She's nothing if not old school. I built my business from the ground up, hustling every step of the way. So, yes. I am the dominant one. The overachiever. The one who doesn't fuck up because she can't. That's probably why Ben grabbing me by the neck toward his luscious lips feels so fucking good.

I can finally let go.

He sucks on my full lower lip and bites it a little. I cover his face with my hands, his scruff making me hotter. I take him all in as he grabs my ass tightly with both hands. My back is pressed against the bathroom door, he lifts me off the floor with his strong hands. Ben slides my thong to one side with his finger and begins to massage my clit with his thumb, as one digit penetrates. I moan, my warm breath on his lips.

"You aren't getting rid of me that easily," Ben groans as he inserts a second digit, pumping them inside of me. He nibbles my neck as his fingers dance a salsa inside of my pussy.

"Who...are...you?" I ask, my pussy getting wetter and wetter.

I suck on his earlobe and he moans. Ben rubs my nub in circles, fast enough to bring me to ecstasy but slow enough to keep me from climaxing.

"Ooooh! Oooh!" I yell, unafraid of who's on the other side of the door.

I want to forget. I want to cum. I want Ben.

His fingers speed up as I pant. My mouth is wide open. My eyes stay on Ben as he presses his forehead against mine. He's going to see me orgasm. I usually tuck my face inside of a man's neck to hide my cum face. But he's going to see me cum. He's going to see me lose control. My body convulses like I'm having a seizure. A euphoric, don't-want-it-to-stop seizure.

"Aaaaaah!' I explode.

My face twists. My body contracts before I collapse inside of Ben's arms. My legs, still straddling him, go limp. He holds them up with the weight of his body and begins massaging my pussy with his fingers again. I whimper with pleasure as he does things with his hands that I've been dreaming of since this morning.

Ben's lips rise into a half smile, his seductive eyes half open as he waits for my typical reaction: to run. Push him away. But today is my party, and I'll do what I want. Today I agreed to be Juan's fake girlfriend. Today I don't care what others think or say when I step out of the bathroom with Ben.

Fuck *el que diran*.

Cat and Mouse

Ben washes his hands while I comb my hair in front of the bathroom mirror. He watches me with a sexy grin as I reapply my red lipstick. I watch him watch me. Goosebumps cover my skin.

"Have dinner with me next week."

He saunters to me, stands behind me, and envelops me in his arms. My cheeks turn red. Ben leans in to kiss my neck. The euphoria from my recent orgasm intermingling with the bubbly I had earlier has officially taken effect.

Shit! Juan. Dominican Republic.

"I...can't," I say quietly.

I stare at our reflection in the mirror and notice Ben's jaw clench. His brows furrowed in frustration.

"Stop running from this," he replies, his tone still relaxed but commanding.

"No, it's not that. I want to try...." I wave my hand over our reflection. "Whatever *this* is."

We do look good together. Our chemistry is insane and he just feels so familiar. I swallow, unsure of how to proceed. Ben tilts his head, still waiting, as cool as a cucumber. I feel the heat returning to my pussy, excited by his laid-back, yet confident demeanor. He's observant. Calm. But strong and decisive. It's intriguing and sexy as hell.

"Babe. I just have another commitment," I admit. I can't blow Juan's cover. I promised.

"Another date?" Ben drops his arms and takes a step back.

How does he know? Is he a *brujo*? Candi would love it if the latter were true. She'd rush to Ben whenever she'd see an angel number. 222 being her favorite.

"It means love and harmony!" she gushes when a car drives by with 222 on the license plate. And God forbid a pigeon shits on her. In Dominican culture, it's a symbol of good fortune. I call bullshit. If that were the case, my relatives would be filthy rich. We live in NYC, for fuck's sake.

"Ben," I start.

"Forget it, boss."

He shrugs his shoulders, pretending he isn't furious. Jealous, even. And it infuriates me. My cheeks burn hotter than my pussy throbbed mere seconds ago. Does he think he owns me because he turned me out twice? I turn around to face him and lean against the sink, crossing my arms across my chest.

"We're not a couple," I say icily.

Ben nods and reaches for the door. He swings it open and walks away without uttering another word. The door shuts. I feel a rush of adrenaline. An urge to chase after him. Instead, I do what I always do in matters of the heart: freeze.

I turn and face my reflection in the mirror.

"Good going, babe."

I smooth out my dress and regain my composure, making my way toward the door to return to my guests.

"Yo?!" I hear Candi yell from the other side.

I wince. "Yes?!"

What did she hear? Did she see Ben storm out? How am I going to explain all of this?

"Why are you in the men's bathroom?" Candi pushes the door open and stands in front of me with a hand on her hip.

"Long line for the girls," I lie.

"You've been here for like 30 minutes." She searches my face for answers. "And I just saw this hottie walk out of here. Like...dude is fiiiiine. A scruffy beard and *everything*." Candi shudders while picturing Ben. Suddenly, an embarrassment look spreads across her face.

She knows.

"Ha!" she pretends to laugh. "J.K. He wasn't that hot. No one is as hot as Joel. Ok. He was fine. Just don't tell Joel I said anything, please? You know how he gets," Candi rattles on.

I nod, promising to keep yet another secret and silently thanking God for Candi's self-absorption.

Juan in a Million

Candi and I move past the crowd that's formed at Vivere.

"See!" Candi squeals, pointing in the direction of the main bar. "That's the guy, Yo!"

"I didn't see him at all. Maybe he just peeked in."

I rush through my sentence hoping Candi believes me. I'll tell her about Ben when I know what's happening between us. If there's more "us" to explain. Suddenly, my heart feels heavy, like I'm heartbroken over a relationship that hasn't even begun. It could be amazing. It feels different. And not just because of the unforgettable orgasms. We're just connected. Which is crazy talk. We barely know each other. Maybe I'm losing my mind. Maybe this is more about Pedro than Ben. Maybe I need a fucking nap.

It doesn't matter anyway. He's done with me.

"Let's get back to the party." I push Candi toward the outside garden. "Joel must miss you."

"Aw, Yo! That was so sweet of you to say."

"Of course. You two are very cute." I smile.

Candi's eyes well up with tears. "You're turning into a softie – and I love it!" She hugs me as tears fall down her face. "I'm just so happy."

"I'm glad, babe. You deserve it."

"You do too, Yo," she says, wiping her tears away. "And maybe you've already met your match."

Candi winks at me. I panic. She knows. She must know.

"What are you talking about?" I nervously look over my shoulder at Ben, who's sipping a drink at the bar while chatting with a Vivere Bottle Girl. My blood boils.

"Juan! He's here and it's time for cake. Yay!"

"Yaaay!" I feign excitement.

Candi grabs me by the hand and pulls me back into the party, taking me directly to Juan. I reach over my shoulder to get another glance at Ben, scanning his surroundings for other women. I watch as the same Bottle Girl strokes his muscular arm. My face burns.

"Candi!" Juan yells above the loud music, bringing me back to Earth. He looks at me with fearful eyes and pulls me in for a hug. We embrace awkwardly.

"I feel the sparks, you guys!" Candi yells, pointing at us so the entire room can witness our budding albeit faux relationship.

"Look how cute they are! My cousin and my best friend!"

Cousin Reina rushes to my side, rolling her eyes at Candi before extending her hand to Juan.

"*Mucho gusto,*" she says sultrily. "Now, Juan. *Mi amor, dime.*" Reina pauses to grab her phone from her fanny pack." Do you know any available, fine, grown-ass men that I can get acquainted with?"

"Oh, I'm sure he knows plenty, Reina!" Candi chimes in, trying to warm up to her. "Don't you cousin?"

Reina ignores Candi, swatting her away like a fly buzzing in her ear. She leans back and raises her eyebrow. "Wait. Haven't I seen you at Q?"

Juan chuckles nervously at the mention of Washington Heights' popular gay club, which Reina frequents with her gay BFF, Antonio. He grabs me by the waist in an attempt to prove his heterosexuality. I cough, nudging him sharply with my elbow. I agreed to help him in the Dominican Republic, not at my birthday party.

"You must have me mistaken," Juan says, convincingly. "Reina, is it?" He takes her hand in his. "I've heard so much about you from Candi. If you're as magnificent as this beauty you call a cousin, you must have many options."

Reina flips her long, jet-black hair with her available hand, excited that a high-value man is giving her attention. "I'm 45 going on 30!" she simpers like a schoolgirl, batting her eyes at Juan.

"Come on, Reina. Let's go to the bar," I say, winking at Candi. She nods in acknowledgment. It's Mission Get Reina Sober and I'm on duty.

***

"But I don't wanna go home!" Reina slurs as I shove her in an Uber.

"Sleep it off, *prima*," I say sternly, wagging my finger in her face.

I strap on her seatbelt, kiss her on the lips, and watch as the Uber turns the corner toward St Nicholas Avenue.

I crack my neck. "What a 24 hours."

I contemplate an escape from all the fuss and muss that is my birthday party. I appreciate it all, but I much rather snuggle in bed with *The Departed*, my favorite Leonardo DiCaprio movie. Fun fact: I am in love with Leo. He's the only white boy who could steal me away from a Dominicano.

"I need to ditch this party," I murmur to myself.

"Let me take you somewhere."

"Ben," I whisper.

I slowly turn around. Our eyes meet and a shiver runs down my spine.

"I have something to show you if you let me."

Ben reaches for my hand and I take it in mine. My heart beats a mile a minute as he takes a step, only inches away from me now.

"And what's that," I whisper shakily, the brisk breeze whipping my hair around my face. Ben takes a strand and tugs it behind my ear.

"The tenderness that you deserve."

I laugh, shaking my head from side to side. "And how do you know what I deserve?"

Ben chuckles. "You don't stop, do you?" He wraps his hands around my waist and tilts his head to the side in contemplation. "I like that about you."

"Do you, now." I smirk, loving our natural banter.

"I do. You're amazing, Yo. Smart and witty. Accomplished. You take care of the people that you love, I can tell. Not to mention..."

My cheeks burn and pussy palpitates with every word he utters.

"You're fucking sexy. The most beautiful woman."

I lay my head on his chest and shut my eyes. He holds me and we stand in silence. I can't shake how safe I feel with him although we've just met. I feel comforted. Seen and heard. I want more of this...more of Ben. Why am I stopping myself?

"I'm scared," I admit out loud.

Ben holds me tighter to reassure me. I lift my head from his chest and smile at him sheepishly, feeling overwhelmed by my sudden vulnerability. He cradles my face in his warm, manly hands and kisses me. I nibble on his lower lip and he moans. We finally come up for air, both beaming.

"Let's go," Ben says, grabbing my hand again.

"But my party..."

I feel the old Yoanna sucking me back into a world of rigidity and responsibility, my fears trying to overpower my desire to take a leap of faith. What has overthinking love ever gotten me? A stale relationship with Pedro, a man who was good on paper and then just dumped me. And now, here I am, standing in front of Ben, who is refreshing and different and sexy in every way. What would happen if I lived in the moment for once in my life? Everything could change. God, I am so ready for change.

"Fuck it!" I shout, throwing all caution to the wind. "I'm in, babe."

This Is Real

I rest my head on Ben's shoulder as we take in the view from Inspiration Point in silence. Although I've lived in Washington Heights and Inwood all of my life, I've never visited this historical landmark reminiscent of a Grecian temple.

"This was designed as a rest stop in 1924 by Gustave Steinacher," Ben breaks the silence.

"It's beautiful," I say while tracing the structure with my fingertips.

"But..." Ben turns to me and holds me by the waist. "It became a lot more than that." His eyes twinkle with mischief.

"And what's that?" I ask curiously.

"Young lovers came up here to do what young lovers do. The police nicknamed them 'auto spooners.'" Ben chuckles at the term.

"How do you know all this?"

"I love history and architecture." He winks.

"Interesting," I muse. "So, is this why you brought me here? To show off your knowledge."

"Maybe." Ben strokes my cheek. "Or maybe it's to 'auto spoon' with you."

I tilt my head back and laugh. Ben smiles from cheek to cheek.

"I love to make you laugh, you know."

"I do now." I blush.

"And for the record, in case it isn't clear... I want to do more than 'auto spoon' with you."

"What else do you want?" My pulse quickens.

"Yoanna. I want to *know* you."

He kisses my forehead and brings me in close. His embrace warms every inch of my skin as the winter wind kicks up and swirls around us.

I look up at Ben, his eyes penetrating every fiber of my being. "Ok."

"You got it, boss."

Ben takes my lips in his. Our tongues mingle, dancing in unison, and I feel a fire in my chest. I've never felt this kind of heat, this kind of passion and intensity. The chemistry between Ben and I feels kismet. Like I was meant to lock us in that stairwell so that we can be right here right now. I nibble on Ben's lips before parting from them. We hold each other close, watching as snow begins to fall.

"Christmas/birthday snow. Ms. Yoanna, are you a witch?" Ben jokes.

"If I'm a witch, I'm not that powerful, babe. My birthday has been officially over," I look at my watch, "as of two hours ago."

"I want to make you feel like it's your birthday every day," Ben says intensely.

"Why?" I ask cautiously. It's hard to break a long-life habit of distrusting people.

Ben throws his hands up, exasperated. He begins to pace alongside the perimeter of the landmark.

"Ben. I'm just cautious. That's my default. Also, I don't know that much about you other than what you shared when we first met. It's unfair of you to expect me to just trust your...."

"Intentions," Ben finishes my sentence.

I sigh. "Yes."

Ben walks over to me. Facing me now, he cups my chin in his hand. "I intend to protect you. And, if you let me, to love you unconditionally."

My eyes well up with tears. I shake my head as they stream down my cheeks. "I'm complicated, Ben."

"I know. I like that. I like that you're stubborn. Strong and willful. I love how confident you are. I love how you cum."

My face turns beet red. I wrap my arms around his neck and cover his face with a flurry of kisses. Our lips meet again. The snow continues to fall, cooling our skin.

"I love how you kiss me," I say breathlessly. "But..."

"You need to know more," Ben mumbles, as he sucks on my lower lip.

"Hmmm...yes," I murmur.

Our lips part. Ben looks deeply into my eyes. "Soon. I'll tell you everything you need to know."

"Just answer one thing. And I'm sorry if it offends you."

Ben nods, permitting me to pry.

"How can you afford to live in my building?"

"Rent control. That apartment has been in my family for decades before being gentrified by hoity toity rich folks like yourself."

"Excuse me," I gasp playfully. "I'm from here. Born and bred in Washington Heights."

Ben laughs. "Oh, I know. Your fancy clothes and money don't fool me."

"And don't you forget it!" I smack him playfully on the chest.

I shiver and Ben holds me tighter. The wind blows harder and the snow falls faster. "Let's get you home."

To the Motherland

I stretch my arms under the covers, my cashmere blanket caressing my skin. My eyes shut tight, I replay last night on a loop. Although we live in the same building, and Ben has tasted my pussy and felt her gush all over his fingers and mouth, we decided to go to our respective homes.

"So it's clear this isn't about sex," Ben murmured in my ear after one more good-night kiss.

I wanted him to come inside. I wanted him inside of me. I still do. Goosebumps scatter all over my body. I shut my eyes tighter. My body craves to feel all of him. To see what he's working with. My hand rubs my chest, fingertips flickering my erect nipple. My breath quickens as I travel south, opening my lips and meeting my bud.

I slowly rub on my nub, breathing heavier now. Imaging Ben plunging into me, I open my legs wider and buck my hips, inserting my finger inside my pussy. I moan, louder, grinding harder.

"Oh Ben," I cry, barely able to catch my breath.

"Ah, ah. Aaaaaaaah!"

Release.

My eyes flutter open when I hear someone banging at my door.

"Coming!"

I throw my blanket off me, grab my phone, and read the flurry of texts from Candi and Joel. Knowing it's them at the door from Candi and Joel's, "We're coming over!" message, I quickly wash my hands in the bathroom and run my fingers through my long tresses. I jog to the door and swing the door open.

"What is going on with you, Yo?" Candi barks, pushing a bag of bagels and bacon toward me.

It's BBM Sunday. I completely forgot.

Joel barges in behind her, his nostrils flaring. "Why do you keep disappearing?"

He sets a Prosecco and a bottle of OJ on the kitchen counter for our mimosas. The M in BBM Sundays.

"I'm not..." I stammer, trying to regain my composure. "I was tired. It's been a long weekend.

"Sis, we didn't even do our usual birthday toast this year. Candi and I went to find you and you were gone." Joel paces, rubbing his head anxiously.

"We were really worried, Yo." Candi's voice cracks. She walks over to me and eyes me quizzically. "I just feel something is happening, but what hurts me more is that you're not telling *me*. I get not telling Joel..."

"Hey! I resent that!" Joel throws a hand towel in our direction. Candi tilts her hips and dodges the attack.

"You know what I mean, Joel," Candi states sternly while surveying my face like an undercover cop.

She turns to face him. "Just give us a minute. Please, my love." In seconds, Candi's voice switches from disciplinarian to sexy lover.

Joel hangs his head in defeat and shuffles over to her. "Anything for you, Candi Cane."

He kisses Candi on the lips and smirks before hiding away in the living room. We hear a basketball game blaring from the television as Candi and I walk into my bedroom. I shut the door behind us, sit down, and pat the spot next to me on the bed.

"I'll tell you everything. I promise, babe."

Candi nods, her naturally big eyes widening as I chronicle the last 48 hours. I tell her about Ben, our walk down the stairs, what we did on Bonita and in Vivere's restroom, and our night at Inspiration Point in Fort Tryon Park. I can hardly believe this is my life.

"It's like a *telenovela*, Yo." Candi beams. "I am so happy for you!"

"It's…unbelievable," I admit. "But I'm scared, Candi. That's why I didn't tell you."

"But you can tell me anything. Always. You know that, Yo. You always have."

I wince. "You don't know everything about Pedro."

Candi blinks rapidly, confused at my sudden revelation. "Did he do something to you? Did he cheat?"

"No, nothing like that. I faked our relationship for a long time. I wasn't happy, babe. Honestly, I'm not really sure I loved him. We just fit in the traditional sense, you know?" Candi tightens her lips and nods in agreement. "And you and Ben? Do you fit in the best way?"

I blush at the mention of his name. "It feels like we do. But that's why I kept this to myself. It's new. Like nothing I've ever experienced before. I needed to figure this out on my own without you or Joel's fantasies about love."

Candi gasps at my use of the L word. "Do you *love* him? Do you love Ben?"

"Is it crazy that I feel like I do? Like, love at first sight?"

I throw myself back on the bed. Tears trickle down my cheeks. Candi snuggles beside me as she often does when needing my wisdom, reassurance, and TLC. Only this time I need her.

"I think you love him, bestie." Candi wraps her arms around me. "And that's amazing."

I sniffle, my hands shaking because I fear I am losing control.

"I hope so, babe."

Busted

"Have a safe trip and an amazing time in Puerto Rico!" Candi hollers out of Joel's car window. They insisted on driving me to JFK airport after I told them I was escaping New York City to attend a gynecological conference in Puerto Rico. There is a conference, I covered my tracks. Candi is very intuitive. She'll investigate and do a Google deep dive when her spidey senses kick in. I hate that I lied, even if it is to protect Juan. Joel felt badly that I was spending the holiday season "alone" after everything that happened with Pedro. Being the bestie that she is, Candi kept my secret about Ben from my twin. So I just told them I needed a distraction before our New Year's festivities.

I wave goodbye and walk through the sliding doors. The airport buzzes with holiday travel, people speed walking and some running to catch their flights. I'm three hours early, no need to rush. I like to people-watch in the Delta Sky Lounge with a Prosseco and a meal.

I grab a seat at the bar and order my drink from the bartender.

Ding!

I look down at my phone and see a text message from Ben.

"Safe flight. I'll miss you."

Butterflies dance a merengue in my tummy. "I'll miss you, too. Be back soon. Only a few days."

"A few days too many. Work will be a good distraction for me," Ben responds.

"I know. This was an unexpected work event. I wish I didn't have to go."

"At least you're working in San Juan. Send me a bikini selfie." Ben sends the googly eyes emoji.

I bite my lip, feeling terrible that I'm lying to Ben so early in our relationship. Oh God, a relationship! I shake my head and chuckle, taking a swig of my Prosecco. We haven't made it official, but at dinner last night we agreed to be exclusive.

***

"It's just you and me," Ben said, splattering kisses all over my hand while we snuggled inside a booth at Lola's, a Cuban restaurant in the Upper West Side.

The night before my flight he insisted on taking me to dinner and our official first date. I like to rest and stay in, packing, organizing, and checking off items from my to-do list before I travel. But Ben didn't need to do much to convince me; a passionate kiss at my doorstep that morning was all it took.

Dinner was amazing. The sirloin steak was tender and moist, just divine. And Ben? He was the man he's always been with me: attentive, a great listener, affectionate, and loving. We dove deeper into our childhoods, our relationships, and what we like to do for fun.

"Pool," Ben and I said simultaneously when sharing our favorite hobby.

I howled, almost spitting out my drink. "Oh my God! What are the odds?"

"I go to a pool hall every week. I'm very good. And competitive." Ben grinned, winking at me in an attempt to bait me.

"I also go to a pool hall every week. A private one. I'm a member." I paused and leaned into Ben, my breasts pressed against his chest. "That's how good *I* am."

"I bet," Ben muttered. "But I'll still win."

He slid his hand around my waist. I cupped his face in my hands. Tender nibbles followed a lustful, open-mouthed kiss for everyone to see.

"Ok. It's just you and me." I agreed.

***

"Gotta go to work. Early shift." Ben texts.

"Have a great day, babe," I reply, flagging the bartender for my second drink.

"Text me when you land in Puerto Rico."

I respond with the lips emoji. Guilt washes over me and I debate whether I should come clean with Ben. Maybe he'll understand why I'm helping Juan by lying about being his girlfriend. I take a sip and look down at my phone in my hands. Or maybe he'll be hurt that I lied to him in the first place. I bite my lip, hesitating on what to do. No. Don't say anything. What he won't know won't hurt him.

I stuff my phone back in my black D&G tote bag and return to people-watching.

***

Merengue ripiao echoes through Santiago's airport as I make my way outside. I can smell *la leña* instantly, the smell of firewood bringing back memories. I'm handed a *Presidente* beer and take a sip. The *merengue* band plays louder as I approach. They encourage me to dance and I sway my hips and laugh. I always feel 10 pounds lighter in the motherland.

"It's good to be home," I whisper to myself.

Although I've never lived outside of New York, Joel and I visited our maternal grandparents with our parents every summer before they moved to New York City themselves. Staying in the city of Santiago gave us first-hand access to restaurants and bars while still being close enough to explore the rural region, including the rivers and lakes of El Cibao, the mountainous area in the northern part of the Dominican Republic.

"Yoanna!"

I turn and see Juan waving, standing beside a black Escalade. The driver walks over to me, grabs my suitcase, and places it in the trunk.

"*Senorita.*" The driver motions that I take the backseat. Before I make my way inside, Juan grabs me in his arms and squeezes me tightly.

"*Mi amor*!" He says loudly. "*Cuanto gusto verte*!"

Juan quickly goes in for a kiss on the lips. My reflexes kick in and I turn my face, giving him my cheek.

"So coy!" Juan laughs nervously, surveying the crowd in case anyone noticed.

"We're fine, Juan," I whisper in his ear. "But don't ever do anything I've never agreed to."

I step back and smile tightly. We're going to have to review the terms of our agreement before The Politicos y Artistas Gala.

An hour later, we arrive in Puerto Plata at the Casa Colonial, a five-star boutique hotel with the best dining and accommodations the island has to offer. The pristine private beach, infinity pools, and master suites are my cup of tea. I'm impressed but not surprised. Juan likes luxury as much as I do; the one benefit of being his beard for the next two days.

"After you, Yoanna." Juan places his hand in mine and I try not to flinch, remembering what I signed up for. We stroll into the elevator. The doors close and I take my hand back immediately.

"Don't you *ever* do that again!" I seethe, facing him with my hand on my hip.

"The kiss..." Juan looks at me apologetically.

"Yes!" I glare at him. "You caught me off guard, babe."

I cross my arms and watch the elevator numbers tick up. "I know I agreed to help you. I'm here. But we need to talk about what this," I motion between us back and forth, "charade looks like in public."

"I'm sorry, Yoanna," Juan says. "We will talk and set whatever parameters you deem fit. I really appreciate you doing this for me." I soften, looking back at him now. His shoulders slouch and he rubs his face, stressed from playing pretend. This successful and larger-than-life man is so defeated.

"I'm here, babe." I rub his back, trying to soothe some of the pressure away. "I'm here."

***

"Yoanna, you look stunning!" Juan gasps.

I strut into the foyer of our master suite donning a red, deep-plunging sequin Dolce gown that hugs every curve and kisses the floor.

"Thank you." I give him a little twirl.

"Let me take a photo of you, *bella*."

I hand my phone to Juan and pose seductively. I texted Ben a selfie earlier while getting dressed and have every intention of sending him this head-to-toe look. He hasn't responded yet; he must be busy working the exclusive, private event he told me about when we dined at Lola's.

"I can't say much. A celebrity thing," Ben said.

"Now I'm intrigued. You have to tell me who."

"Sorry, boss. Server/client confidentiality." Ben winked.

I smile at the memory, forgetting where I am for a second.

"Who were you just thinking about?" Juan teases. Snapping more photos of me and of us as we walk to the elevator.

"No one," I say, not wanting to get into it. "Let's get this show on the road."

Juan beams, his gratitude showing, and hooks my arm in his. We take the elevator, arrive at the lobby, and walk outside the hotel. We're immediately bombarded with flashing lights from Dominican paparazzi.

"Juan! Juan! *Quien es tu novia*?" A photographer shouts as we make our way to the trolly taking us to Casa Colonial's Lucia Restaurant.

"Yoanna!" I call, playing my part.

Juan takes my hand in his and kisses it before helping me inside our ride. He pauses and smiles for a photo before climbing in beside me. We wave like Princess Diana and Prince Charles and head to the event.

"How do you feel?" Juan asks.

"I'm good. How are you? I know that's not easy. Pretending all the time." I pat his hand.

"It isn't, but I'm not ready to be honest about who I am. Besides, I'm used to it." He shrugs and my heart breaks for him and the secret he holds.

Minutes later, the trolley stops. More photographers snap their shots while we pose outside the step and repeat. Finally finished, we make our way inside the venue.

"Freeze!" A man shouts.

Startled, Juan stumbles on my dress' train and falls back. I'm pushed to the side by one of his bodyguards when a flurry of men in blue move in on Juan and place him in handcuffs.

"*Usted está bajo arresto.*" A police officer tells Juan.

"What's happening? *¿Que paso?*" I ask the bodyguard who is holding me back.

"*No se,*" he says, watching the cops walk Juan to a police car.

"*Dejame.*" I release myself from his grasp and hurry over to the dozens of police officers on the scene.

"*¿Que esta pasando?*" I call, hoping to get answers to help Juan. There has to be some mistake.

"Yoanna."

Ben, dressed in blue slacks and a cream linen shirt, faces me.

"What are you doing here? How did you know..." I notice a holster around his waist with a gun tucked inside.

"Who are you?" I demand with gritted teeth. I search his face for an explanation.

Ben presses his lips tightly and looks down at his feet. "I'm sorry, Yoanna. I didn't mean for you to get involved in this."

"In what?" I feel a blinding migraine coming on.

"Again. Who. The fuck. Are you?" My chest heaves, waiting for his response. For some explanation that differs from what I think this is.

"I'm an undercover cop, Yo. I can't go into specifics right now." He looks back at the police squad. "But I will. Soon."

My eyes well up with tears. "Forget my number. Forget me."

"Yoanna," Ben says softly.

He reaches for my shoulder. I cringe and wipe away a tear.

"We are done."

It's Always Been You

"**H**oy. *Si*." I speak to the airline over the phone while quickly packing my clothing and toi-letries. "*Gracias*."

I hang up the call, grab my suitcase, and rush to the elevator. If I hurry, I can catch the next flight to New York City and leave this mess behind. The elevator doors open.

"No!" I yell as Ben appears.

"I'm here to get you out of here." Ben approaches me slowly, like a lion tracking his prey.

"I'm not going anywhere with you!"

I try to dodge him but he matches my steps. Ben comes in closer and pulls me into his arms. I try to fight him off, wiggling in his arms, but he's stronger than I am.

"Calm down, Yo. I'm trying to keep you safe."

Ben holds me tighter. I keep fighting back, smacking his chest with the little bit of energy I have left.

"Leave me alone," I sob, tears blinding me.

Ben kisses the wetness. My body goes stiff. He doesn't stop, meeting his lips with mine. I cry into them as we kiss.

"It's not what it looks like," he mutters between nibbles and sucks. "You're a cop. You lied to me." I glare at Ben with a mix of lust, confusion, and anger.

"I know," Ben whispers, kissing my cheeks, nose, and forehead. "I'm sorry. I was undercover. I didn't expect to meet you, to get stuck with you in the stairwell. You weren't supposed to be involved, Yo."

I sniffle. "Please. Go."

"No."

Ben kisses me deeper. My pussy pulsates with every touch. I melt into him. He leads me to the bedroom, rubbing my ass as we walk and kiss and suck. I moan when he rubs my pussy over my thong and licks every inch of my neck. Ben unzips my sundress. It drops to the ground by the foot of the bed. He softly kisses my cleavage and unsnaps my bra, sucking and flicking my nipples with his tongue. I arch my back, enjoying every second. Ben lays my naked body on the bed. I watch, my chest heaving from desire, as he unbuttons his shirt, drops his pants and briefs, and exposes his hard member. It's standing at attention for me.

Ben saunters over to me. I begin touching myself, rubbing my nub, and anticipating his arrival. He gets on his knees and spreads my legs open. His tongue enters me. I grind into him as he dives in.

"Oh, Ben," I whimper, his fingers maneuvering my pussy.

"You're so wet," Ben moans, licking my clit.

He climbs on top of me and I open my legs wider. He penetrates. I cry out with desire as he pumps, his pelvis moving in perfect rhythm with mine. Stroke after stroke, I pant with desire, grabbing his ass, scratching his back, and pushing him in deeper. Ben grinds into me passionately, slowly at first.

"Yoanna," he whispers, his eyes on mine the entire time. "You feel better than I imagined."

I press my lips on his, interlacing with his tongue and sucking on his lower lip, as he pumps faster. He flips me on top and I swerve my hips. My tits bounce. I arch my back, leaning back enough to expose my bud. Ben rubs it slowly.

"Aaah! Don't stop!" I groan, my hips moving faster.

"You're not coming yet," Ben says wickedly, taking his finger away and changing positions.

Spooning me now, he grabs my breast, flicks my nipples, and thrusts into me. I rub my clit faster, getting closer to orgasm the deeper and faster he penetrates. Ben softly bites my shoulder before turning my face toward him with his hand. He pumps faster now, our eyes remaining locked. I pant, breathing heavily as I roll my hips into his. My muscles tighten. My clit swells. I'm ready to burst. I whimper uncontrollably. Ben takes note and picks up the pace. His unrelenting tempo brings me to the peak.

"Oooh!" I gasp.

The heat rises from my pulsating pussy to my bones. I feel a fire within. A fire in my abdomen and in between my legs, burning hotter and hotter. I cry out, my body in flames, bucking and twitching. I go limp in Ben's arms, his eyes still on mine. He rotates my body to face him.

"I love you, Yo," Ben murmurs, stroking my cheek with his fingertips.

"I love you, too."

Ben kisses me on the lips. "Good."

"We still have a lot to talk about," I warn. "You broke my trust." My eyes tear up again.

"I know. I promise I'll tell you everything on the flight back home. And I'm sorry again. The investigation was ongoing. I couldn't– "

"I get it. In my world, it's doctor/patient confidentiality." I nuzzle my head in his neck and breathe him in.

"I can tell you this now. I was undercover as a server to track Juan's business affairs."

"Ok," I say quietly.

Ben scoots down to meet my gaze. "I wasn't there looking for you, but I'm so glad you found me."

Arrival

"Ready to get grilled, officer?" I slide my hand in Ben's and nudge him playfully on the shoulder.

"I was born ready." He winks, leaning in for a quick kiss before the big reveal.

I slide open the doors and we stroll in, hand in hand. I scan the hall for Candi and Joel and catch them necking behind the coat rack.

"There they are." I point to the handsy couple.

"Smart," Ben muses.

"What?" I ask, confused.

"Their makeout spot. That'll be us next." His eyes are ablaze, they wander over my lips and land on my cleavage.

I giggle, excited for what he has in store. Life with Ben has been an adventure from the moment we met. Once he could legally divulge his role in Juan's arrest and, later, his release, I understood his position. I respected it even. As an undercover cop, he has to protect and serve, and that also means withholding information from those he loves. It hurt me deeply and almost blew up my life and our relationship, but neither of us meant for this to happen. For *us* to happen.

***

"I was assigned to work undercover at your Christmas Eve event. We got a tip that Juan and his business partner would be there," Ben explained on the flight back to New York City. "Juan's partner has been smuggling drugs through Juan's vendors."

"Babe!" I gasped at the news. "Did you find anything?"

"I did," Ben admitted. "I went to the stairwell to call for backup, but then you showed up." He grabbed my hand and squeezed it. "I got distracted. And locked out. By the time we were...done." Ben nips at my lower lip and I feel a buzz in my belly. "He was gone."

"I'm so sorry! I almost jeopardized your job!"

"Don't apologize. We caught him. It all worked out. And this...us...it's worth all the losses."

I kiss Ben passionately, shamelessly devouring him in front of everyone without a care in the world.

"I love you," he says between nibbles.

"I love you, too."

***

"You!" Candi yells at Ben, stomping over to him and pointing her finger in his direction.

"We can still run," I joke.

"I can handle it." Ben stands tall, gripping my hand tighter as he faces Candi's scowl. Joel stands behind her, letting my bestie have her moment before he gives Ben the obligatory, brotherly third degree.

"You arrested my cousin. *Mi familia*!" She smacks Ben lightly on the chest. "Oh, no! Shit. You're a cop. Please don't arrest me!" Candi pleads, realizing her mistake.

"Hi Candi, I'm Ben. I've heard a lot about you," Ben chuckles.

"But you released him," Candi continues slowly. "So.. thank you, officer." She gives him a little salute.

"Now it's my turn." Joel steps forward, his chest puffed like a rooster. "What are your intentions with my sister?"

"I love her," Ben says matter-of-factly. "I intend to love her as long as she lets me."

I blush, fighting back tears. "Joel. He's good. We're good," I say, talking my twin down.

"As long as you're happy, sis," Joel replies. "Then I'm happy." A smile spreads across his face, exposing his dimples, and he goes in for a hug.

"Welcome to the family, Ben!" Joel and Ben get into a bro hug while Candi rushes into my arms.

"I am so happy for you."

"I can't believe this is my life," I admit, hugging my best friend tighter.

"Believe it," Ben says, hugging me from behind and kissing me on the neck.

I smile, overwhelmed with the feeling of pure joy and love that surrounds me. Ben surprises me at every turn. And for the first time in my life, I don't need to know it all. I don't want to know what's next. I want to live and love freely even if it's not safe.

Epilogue: Reina

"*Wepa!*" I shake my round ass in the middle of the dance floor surrounded by strangers without a care in the world. "That's my shit!"

My shoulders bop to Fatman Scoops old school club mix. "You got a 100 dollar bill, get your hands up! You got a 50 dollar bill, get your hands up!"

I take a sip of my drink, careful not to spill over my new, pleather bodysuit. It fits tight enough that it hugs me in all the right places...thick thighs, big breasts, and all. My back and waist look a little lumpy thanks to my love handles. But it's my body. I'll stuff myself into a bodysuit like a sardine in a can if I want to.

"Heyyyyyyy!" I wave at my friend, Elena, who I haven't seen since we arrived at the Copa an hour ago. She's been grinding with a particular guy since checking our coats, leaving me on the dance floor to fend for myself.

"Reina! *Muchacha*!" Elena dances over.

"Where's your boo?" I ask, a hint of jealousy in my voice.

"Somewhere." She waves over the crowd. "You know no man can lock me down!" She laughs, grinding her hips to the music. "Girl, I'm so glad you came out tonight. It's been too long."

I nod in agreement. I just recently re-entered the club scene after breaking up with Peter, my high school sweetheart and the father of my 10-year-old son, Michael. Elena is my long-time friend. We met at this very club 15 years ago when Peter and I were on another break. Our M.O. then was to party till the lights came on and our feet hurt so badly that we'd have to dance barefoot. We were always the last ones on the dance floor.

Elena and I aren't necessarily tight, but we've created so many memories right here. Especially as each other's wing women. That is until I got back with Peter for the 100th time months after meeting her. Even though Peter cheated on me more times than a DJ interrupts a song, I took him back year after year. We were high school sweethearts and he's my baby daddy. I loved him deeply, but he just couldn't keep it in his pants.

That's over. I'm here on the prowl with Elena who refuses to settle down.

"What you been up to?" Elena asks, scanning the crowd for both eligible and ineligible men.

She's not one to care about labels and has been a mistress a time or two. As someone who's been cheated on consistently, her nonchalant attitude about monogamy bugs me, but Elena is the only friend from my old crew who is still single and down to party.

"Just being a single mom," I shout over Fat Man Scoop. "Don't leave much time for the club, you know?"

"Right, right." Elena nods while swaying her hips to the music. "And you're finally done with that asshole?"

"Done. *Se termino.*"

"*Gracias a Dios*!" Elena throws her hands up and begins to sing along to the song. "I never knew there was a love like this before!"

"All the good-looking women sing along!" I sing back.

"Listen, I get it. Peter is fiiiine. If you weren't my girl..." Elena smirks, swerving her hips to simulate sex. I fight the urge to punch her in her smug face.

"Getting a drink!" I yell, pointing toward the bar.

"Bet!" Elena responds.

A man in his 20s comes in between us, grabbing Elena by the hand and ignoring me completely. Elena twerks on his crotch. I stomp toward the bar, still furious at her for insinuating she'd fuck Peter and fearing the possibility that it's already happened. My blood boils with a mix of anger, anxiety, and jealousy. She's always gotten all of the attention. Even at 38 years old, she's still easily picking up men at the club every weekend.

"And then there's me…" I mutter to myself, finding a spot at the crowded bar. I look around at the surrounding faces.

"Youths." I frown, feeling older than I'd like to. Even at 45, I believe that I'm still full of life, but coming here tonight reminds me that I'm a middle-aged, out of shape, single woman with no prospects.

"A shot of Don Julio!" I yell at the bartender.

Instead of taking my order, he ignores me and continues flirting with the 20-something-year-old next to me.

I slam a $20 bill on the bar. "Don Julio!" I shout again. He glances at me, grabs the money, and stays put.

"Yo!" I growl, my temper flaring. "You're yelling in my ear," the *chiquita* next to me remarks, rolling her eyes. She's so fucking tiny I could bounce her out of this club with just my hip. One hit and she'll go flying.

"I don't give a fuck," I seethe. She backs down. I may be five-foot-tall but my anger is larger than life.

"She said she wants a Don Julio." I hear a man's voice boom over Marc Anthony's, "Mala." The bartender looks up at the man standing behind me and nods. I can feel him pressed up against me. I want to take a peek, but it would be difficult to turn around without rubbing his crotch with my big ass. "Sorry," he leans in and whispers in my ear, acknowledging our physical predicament. "Not a lot of space here."

I crank my neck to look up at him, and I'm met with rich, milk chocolate skin and soulful, russet eyes.

"Hi," he says in a husky voice.

"Hi." I blink rapidly. "Are you real?"

He laughs amusingly, his shoulders shaking.

"I'm Abel."

"Reina," I say breathlessly.

"Don Julio!" The bartender whips me back into reality. "You're short."

"Yeah, I know. Five feet."

The crowd roars as the DJ announces tonight's salsa band.

"I don't care, lady. You're short. You owe me 20 bucks not including tip." The bartender sneers.

It's been so long since I've been dancing, I didn't realize how expensive drinks are now. I frantically search through my fanny pack for more money as people squeeze me on every side to get to the stage.

"There."

I slam the money in front of me, take back my shot, and exhale, ready to feast my eyes on Abel. I swing around with a smile, but he's gone. People begin to gather in front of me, obstructing my view, as the band takes the stage. On tippy toes, I crank my neck to spot him amongst the crowd.

"There he is," I mumble, recognizing his pink and blue striped tee.

"Excuse me," I shout, bumping people with my wide hips and ignoring their glares as I hit them.

"You can do this, Reina." I pump myself up, getting closer now. "You're beautiful. You got this."

I stand behind him and clear my throat before tapping him on the shoulder. He turns around and is standing hand in hand with Elena.

Thank You

Thank you for reading *Heights of Love: Yoanna*! If you enjoyed this book, I would be grateful if you could leave a review on Amazon. Reviews help boost book sales. As an indie author, they are especially helpful! Also, stay tuned for *Reina*, the third novella in the "Heights of Love" series.

Love,
Sujeiry

Heights of Love Series

Download a free bonus scene featuring Candi and Joel: https://dl.bookfunnel.com/y7jph07ih3

Buy *Heights of Love: Candi,* the first book of the series on Amazon: https://amzn.to/3CzYeBD

Stay in the loop by signing up to my newsletter: http://subscribepage.io/4hVnyN

About the Author

Sujeiry Gonzalez is a Dominican American romance author, journalist, and poet, and the co-founder of Corner of Press publishing. Her spicy and often funny romance novels predominantly feature Latinx characters and capture the essence of Dominican culture in NYC. A former relationship journalist and columnist coined, "The Latina Carrie Bradshaw," her articles and stories have been published in *Latina Magazine, Cosmopolitan, Hip Latina, Well + Good*, and many other publications. Sujeiry also hosted Love Sujeiry, a relation-

ship talk radio show, on SiriusXM. Raised in the neighborhood of Washington Heights in NYC, she now resides
on Long Island, NY with her son.

www.ingramcontent.com/pod-product-compliance
Lightning Source LLC
Chambersburg PA
CBHW060336310726

48976CB00007B/2572